LUCKY

Gus Clarke

Kane/Miller
BOOK PUBLISHERS

Hello. I'm Lucky.

I've got plenty to eat,

a roof over my head,

a comfortable bed,

and lots of friends.

We all have.

We all came here for different reasons.

I'm not sure why I came, but I'm glad I did.

Bernard hoped he wouldn't be here long.
But he knows he won't be going home now.

Jim and Edna look after us. They're very good. Sometimes they bring people around to see if we'd like to go and live with them.

Bernard says he hasn't found the right person yet.

But Molly did.

And so did Spike.

Here come some more people.
I wonder if Bernard will like these ones.

No. But Buster did!

Poor Bernard. I know he'd like to find someone to go home with. He's getting a bit too old for all this excitement.

I have an idea! I'll tell the others. They're sure to understand.

Here they come. Chins up, Bernard! Give them a smile.

That's nice!

Oh well, fingers crossed…

Well done, Walter.

Nice one, Nick.

Good girl, Gertie.

Bad boy, Ben. (That's brilliant!)

I think it worked!

Goodbye, Bernard. We'll miss you.
I wonder if *I'll* ever find someone.

But then again...

...I might just stay!